James & the Giant Peach

ROALD DAHL

Disney's

James & the Giant Peach

LANE SMITH · KAREY KIRKPATRICK

Disney PRESS

New York

Printed in the United States of America.

First Edition

1 3 5 7 9 10 8 6 4 2

The artwork for each picture is prepared using oils on board.

This book is set in 18 point Berhard Modern.

Designed by Molly Leach, New York, New York

Library of Congress Catalog Information is available for this title.

ISBN: 0-7868-3105-7 (trade)

ISBN: 0-7868-5039-6 (library)

Foreword

First and foremost—we would like to
acknowledge Roald Dahl. If he hadn't sat down
back in 1961 and put his fantastic ideas of a
lonely boy, some huge bugs, and a giant peach
down on paper, there would be no movie and
there would be no picture book based on the
movie. When books are adapted for film many
changes occur and a new version of the story
often emerges. This book is a reflection of that
process. At its heart, however, it is and always
will be—Dahl.

—L. S. & K. K.

This is James Henry Trotter. He lived in a house by the sea with his loving mother and father. It was their lifelong dream to sail to New York City and climb all the way to the top of the Empire State Building. But one day a terrible thing happened. An angry rhinoceros that had escaped from the zoo gobbled up his poor mother and father in thirty-five seconds flat. At least that's what James was told by his two wicked aunts, skinny Aunt Spiker and fat Aunt Sponge. He was sent to live in their horrible house on the hill where he did nothing but work all day long. Still…he never stopped hoping, and he never stopped dreaming.

One day, while trying to stay out of his aunts' way, he met a Mysterious Old Man who gave him a bag of magic green things. "Take them," the Old Man whispered, "and marvelous things will happen." But James tripped and spilled the green things beneath the barren old peach tree at the top of the hill. All hope was lost, he thought. But on the highest branch of the tree, the tree that had never grown a single leaf, a peach blossomed.

And it grew…and grew…and GREW.

Within minutes it was the size of a house. Aunts Spiker and Sponge wanted the giant peach for themselves, but James was so hungry he took a bite of it. When he did, a large hole appeared in its side.

James was curious, so he crawled in.

GLOWWORM   CENTIPEDE   SPIDER

And there he was, slipping and sliding on the gushy fruit until he
found himself right inside the pit, surrounded by six large bugs!
"Look how frightened you are, dearie," said the kind Ladybug.
"No need for all that," the Old Green Grasshopper added.
"We're your friends." They, like James, hated life on that miserable hill.
"I say we make a break for it!" proclaimed the boastful Centipede.
So he chewed through the stem . . .

LADYBUG   EARTHWORM   GRASSHOPPER

...and away they rolled.

Spiker and Sponge tried to escape in their car, but the giant peach rolled right over it, flattening the automobile like a pancake. And the peach didn't stop there. It kept rolling; right through a village, over a church, and smashing through a fence, carrying it away. Finally, the peach launched itself off a huge cliff and ...

KER-PLUNK! was all they heard when they landed.

They didn't know where they were.

Maybe they didn't want to know, because ...

…they were in the middle of the ocean.

"A most intriguing predicament.
Where shall we go from here?"
asked the Grasshopper.
"To New York City!" James exclaimed.
"My father said it's the city where dreams come true."

But the question was: how do you get a giant peach all the
way across the ocean, especially when there's a huge,

man-eating shark bearing down on you?

 "Shark!?" shrieked the Earthworm. "What do we do now?"

It was James who thought of the idea. Attaching the peach to a hundred seagulls, that is. But everyone did their part to make it happen. The Spider provided the string, the others fought off the shark, and the Earthworm put his neck on the line, allowing himself to be used as bait. One after the other, the seagulls swooped down from the sky. James lassoed them all, and much to the crew's amazement, it worked! The peach began to rise out of the water.

Into the air they soared, narrowly escaping
the jaws of the angry shark.

The Centipede steered the peach majestically through
the endless sky, carried on the wings of one hundred
screeching seagulls. But as they flew, James and the
others began to realize they were ravenously hungry.
And growing hungrier by the minute.

"What do we do?"
cried the worrywart Earthworm.
"We're all going to starve."

James chuckled, "No one's going to starve. Our whole ship is made of food." Indeed it was. Enough food for ten voyages. It was James to the rescue again as he hoisted up handfuls of dripping, juicy peach and fed them to his famished friends. They had never, in all their lives on the hill, tasted anything so delectable, so delicious, so mouthwateringly scrumptious as that fantastic peach.

That night the Spider wove a special web for James to sleep in. It was the softest place he had laid his head in a very long time. But James couldn't shake one fearful thought. "Spiker and Sponge will come after me, won't they?" he asked the Spider. "They'll send the rhino to come and get me." The Spider tenderly stroked the hair from James's forehead. "No one can do anything to you if you do not let them. Now close your eyes. It is time for sleep."

When you sleep you dream. And James was having a perfect dream about life with his new bug friends. But as some dreams do, this one turned itself around. Spiker and Sponge appeared like demons in the sky, swirling round his head and cackling,

"You can't get away from us, you disgusting little worm!"

And they exploded into a shower of sparks and white ashes that rained down on poor James. He bolted awake. The air was cold and crisp. Tiny snowflakes drifted down through the open hatchway above. Snow? he thought to himself. Where on earth could we be?

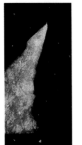 **"This poor excuse for a pilot fell asleep at the helm!"** barked the Grasshopper, pointing an angry finger at the Centipede "We've drifted into frigid Arctic waters."

Down below, they could see the remnants of ships that had drifted this way, never to return.

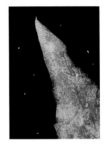

"We're lost," cried the Earthworm. "We'll never find our way out of this without a compass."

Surely one of the sunken ships would have a compass, James thought, but only a fool would jump in to retrieve it.

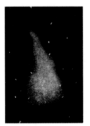 KER-PLOOSH! They heard a splash. The Centipede had jumped overboard! "He'll die down there," shouted James. "I have to go after him."

"Not alone," said the Spider. "Get on my back." James climbed on and the two of them descended into the water, sinking slowly into the murky depths, tied to the peach by the Spider's thin, strong thread.

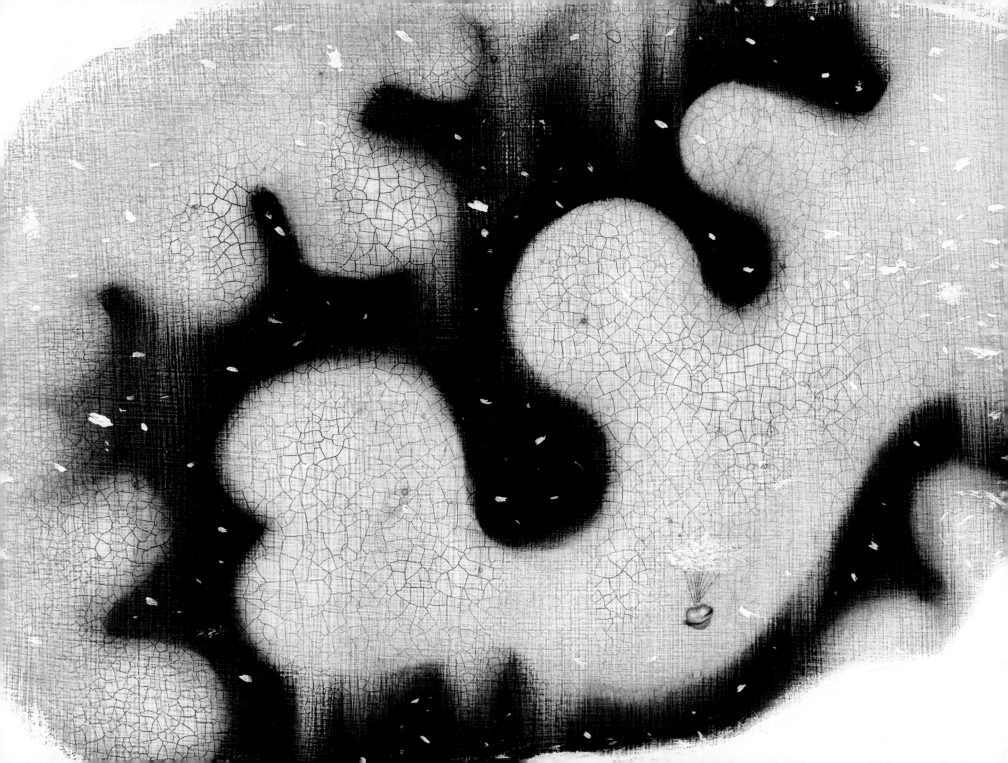

Down . . .
 down . . .
  down they drifted,

through the chilly waters amid the sunken ships that littered the ocean floor. James was more frightened than he had ever been. What if they never made it out? What if they froze to death?

He could swear he saw the faces of his evil aunts, taunting him.

"Stupid foolish dreamer," rang the voices in his head. "Give us back our peach!"

James wondered if they really were following him.

Meanwhile, the Centipede tiptoed aboard one of the sunken ships and found a shiny, gold compass. In an instant he found himself **surrounded by a gang of angry skeletons.**

Just as they were about to

stretch him limb from limb,

James and the Spider swooped down from above.

With the mob of skeletons hot on their trail, they narrowly escaped to the peach with the compass in hand.

They were back on course, sailing straight to New York City through the midnight sky with the Old Green Grasshopper at the helm. James could not help but feel sad that he would arrive there alone, without his mother and father.

Then he heard music—violin music.

It was coming from the Grasshopper, and it was the most comforting sound James had ever heard.

The lilting melody lured the others to the top of the peach, where they gathered around their saddened little friend.

"We're family," they assured him, "and as long as we're around, you will never be alone again."

At that moment, the clouds parted and a
magical city appeared in the distance below.

"New York!" they exclaimed.

But before they could make their descent, the parting clouds formed into
fierce, angry Cloud-Men that swarmed through
the sky, encircling the peach.

The wicked Cloud-Men filled their
cottony cheeks with air and
B L E W!

The resulting wind was as fierce as a hurricane, and it sent
the peach tumbling through the sky.

James watched in fear as the Cloud-Men swirled and
churned and transformed into his worst nightmare, an angry
rhinoceros that galloped
through the air toward the peach.

They all climbed into the rigging for safety, but James slipped and fell onto the fence that had wrapped around the peach. When he stood up, he found himself face to face with the angry rhino. Filled with newfound courage, he pointed a finger at the snorting beast and cried,

"You're just a lot of smoke and noise. And I'm not afraid of you anymore."

At that moment, the rhino exploded.

James clung to the fence as it unwrapped and whipped around the peach, slicing through the strings attached to the seagulls.

The seagulls were whisked away by the fierce wind.

And so were the bugs.

James clutched the stem of the peach as it plummeted
towards the ground. He could only watch as the Ladybug,
the Centipede, the Spider, the Earthworm, the Glowworm, and
the Old Green Grasshopper disappeared into the dark night sky.

BLAM! James landed and landed hard. But where?

On top of the Empire State Building, that's where.
James was in New York City!

A huge crane lowered James and the giant peach
to the street, where throngs of people awaited.
It was all very exciting.
But where were his bug friends?
Why weren't they there to share this moment with him?

Then something horrible happened. Something hideous.
Something absolutely horrendous.

Spiker and Sponge arrived.

They were so angry, they had driven their mashed car all the way across the ocean to take James—and the peach—back to that hideous house on the hill.

"I won't go!" James declared.
"Not me and not the peach!"

The aunts were furious, but before they could do any harm, the bugs appeared in the sky!

They flew to the rescue and wrapped the wicked aunts in a giant cocoon.

A deafening cheer rang through the streets of New York City as scores of children rushed to get a bite of the delicious giant peach.

They ate that peach all the way down to the pit and set it up in Central Park as a permanent home. People of all ages came pouring in just to see it and to hear the tales of James and the bugs' magnificent adventures. And James Henry Trotter, who once was the saddest and loneliest little boy you could find, now had all the friends in the world.

ACKNOWLEDGMENTS

Most of the illustrations in this book were created with the support and collaboration of several talented people behind the scenes of *James and the Giant Peach*, especially the film's director, Henry Selick, whose vision it was to turn the beloved Dahl classic into a movie in the first place. Also thanks to production designer Harley Jessup, Bonita DeCarlo, Jerome Ranft, Bill Boes, and Kendal Cronkhite. The story evolved with the help of many folks. Along with Henry, we'd like to thank all the guys in the story department: Joe Ranft, Kelly Asbury, Pete Von Sholly, Jorgen Klubien, Mike Cachuela, and Mike Mitchell. Also, Jonathon Roberts, Stephen Bloom, David Vogel, Jake Eberts, Denise DiNovi, Brian Rosen, Jeff Bynum, Lenny Young, Chris Montan, Randy Newman, the animators, and the entire cast and crew. A very special thank-you to Liccy Dahl, Amanda Conquy, and Donald Sturrock for their support, to Nada for encouragement, and to Denise Rottina for getting us there and back.

—L. S. & K. K.